THE
WIZARD KING

& Other Spellbinding Tales

for Emrys, with love — J. M.
for Clare and Rowan — C. M.
for Frank and Hannah — J. P.

Barefoot Collections
an imprint of

Barefoot Books
41 Schermerhorn Street, Suite 145
Brooklyn, New York
NY 11201-4845

Graphic design by Judy Linard
Color reproduction by Unifoto, South Africa
Printed and bound in Singapore by Tien Wah Press (Pte) Ltd.

ISBN 1 901223 84 1
Library of Congress Cataloging-in-Publication Data is available upon request
1 3 5 7 9 8 6 4 2

THE
WIZARD
KING

& Other Spellbinding Tales

Retold by John & Caitlin Matthews
Illustrated by Jenny Press

BAREFOOT BOOKS

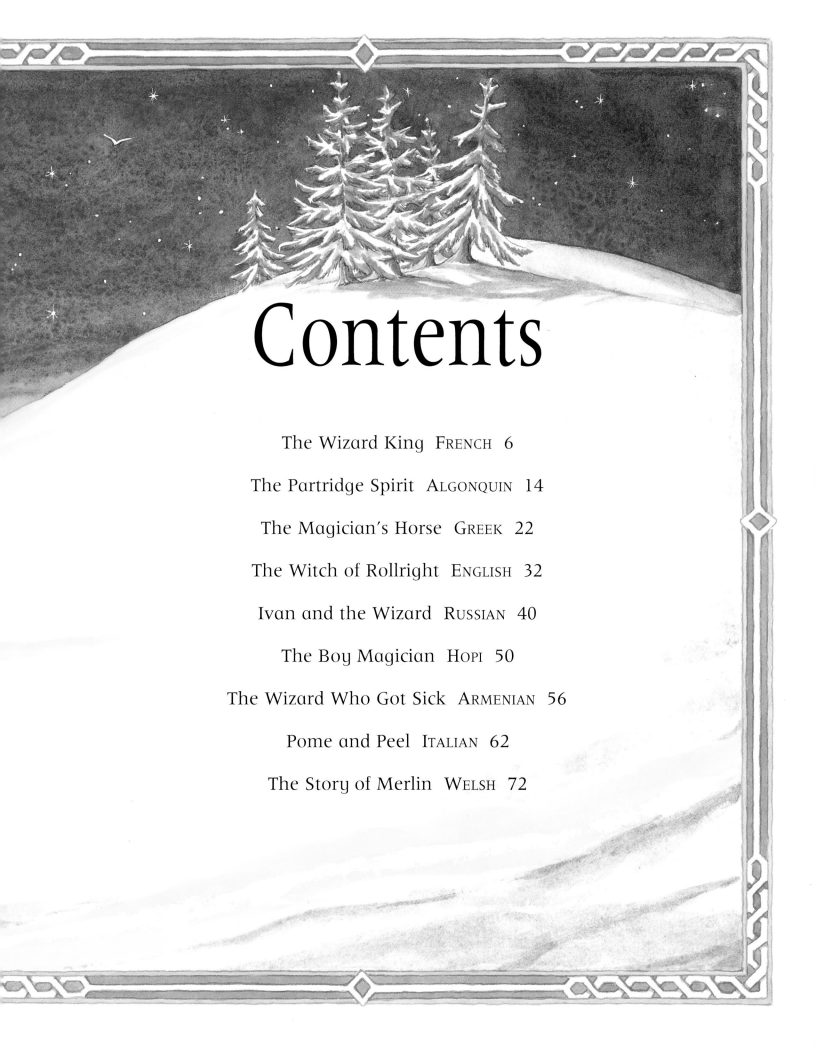

Contents

The Wizard King

FRENCH

There was once a king who was also a very powerful wizard. When the time came for him to marry he chose a wife who was as clever as she was beautiful and he loved her greatly. Soon she gave birth to a beautiful child, a boy, who was the apple of his father's and his mother's eyes.

But the queen had a secret. As a child, she had been entrusted into the care of a fairy godmother, who watched over her ever after. She could not tell the wizard king about this because, as everyone knows, there has always been great rivalry between fairies and wizards, and the queen did not want to make her husband angry.

So, when the baby was only a few weeks old, she took him in secret to visit the fairy, who blessed him with two gifts: the power of pleasing everyone he met, and the power of learning everything he was taught with the greatest ease. The little prince grew into a handsome young man, as clever as he was popular.

Then when he was nineteen-years-old his mother, the queen, died quite suddenly. The prince was heartbroken but his grief was nothing to that of

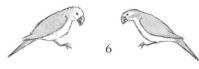

his father. The wizard king was inconsolable. Everywhere he looked he saw things that reminded him of the queen. And so he decided to travel to distant lands, so that he might see nothing but new and unfamiliar things. Changing himself into an eagle, he flew far and wide over land and sea.

Then one day he came to a most wonderful country where the sun always seemed to shine and the scent of jasmine filled the air. The wizard king flew down and settled in the topmost branches of a tall tree. All around him stretched the most beautiful gardens, filled with rare flowers and fountains that shot great jets of silvery water into the air.

There, floating on the surface of an artificial lake, was a golden barge and in the barge sat the most beautiful princess the wizard king had ever seen. He fell in love with her at once, and without a further thought he flew down in his eagle's form and, gripping her in his huge talons, carried her off. The princess cried and cried, and struggled and struggled, but the wizard king flew onward until he was in sight of his own land. There he landed in the midst of a flowery meadow and turned himself back into his own shape.

"Do not weep, I beg you," he said. "I have brought you here to be my queen and to rule over my kingdom with me. My only wish is to make you happy."

But the princess began to weep all the harder. "If you truly want to make me happy," she cried, "take me home."

The wizard king only looked at her sadly and said, "I shall care for you always. You will be happy in time."

Then he took the form of an eagle again and carried the princess to a place near his own palace. There, with his magic, he made a wonderful dwelling for her, a tower of ivory and glass, beautifully furnished. And he summoned maidens to wait upon her, a wonderful talking parrot to entertain her and the finest food that was ever seen. Then he left her, for in his heart he believed that, in time, she would grow to love him.

Every day the wizard king visited the princess, bringing her gifts and speaking kind and gentle words to her. But there were no doors in the tower, and the princess knew that she was a prisoner. So she felt only hatred for the wizard king, and longed to be set free. At first the wizard king was patient, but as time passed and the princess remained as cold and sad as the day he had brought her home, he began to grow suspicious. "Perhaps," he thought, "she has seen my son, who is so handsome and accomplished. She must have fallen in love with him."

So the wizard king decided to send his son away to travel and learn more of the world outside his father's kingdom. The prince set out with great excitement, for he loved to see new places. He traveled through many kingdoms, until he came to the very one from which the wizard king had stolen the princess. The king and queen of that land made him most welcome, but they could not hide the sorrow they felt at the loss of their beloved daughter.

Then one day, when the prince was visiting the queen in her own rooms, he saw a portrait hanging on the wall. At once he asked who the beautiful girl in the picture was and, with tears in her eyes, the queen told him it was the princess who had been carried off by a great eagle.

The prince swore that he would not rest until he had found the lost princess for, if the truth be known, he had fallen in love with her. The queen promised that if he succeeded he would get her daughter's hand in marriage, and half the kingdom as well.

The prince set out, carrying with him a miniature portrait of the princess. He went straight to the fairy under whose protection his mother had placed him. She listened to the prince's story and went to consult her magic books. When she came back she said, "It was your own father who carried off the princess. She is nearby, imprisoned in a tower, surrounded by a magical mist. It will be very hard to get through."

"What can I do?" asked the prince.

The fairy thought for a while, then she said, "The princess has a wonderful talking parrot in her tower. It is the only thing, except for the wizard king, that is allowed to come and go as it pleases. It often flies this way. I will catch it and use my magic to turn you into the shape of the parrot. That way you can visit the princess and no one will ever know."

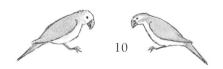

Everything turned out as the fairy planned. She caught the parrot the next time it left the tower and shut it in a golden cage. Then the prince, in the shape of the bird, flew through the magical mist and entered the tower.

The princess was every bit as beautiful as her portrait. The prince was so dazzled that he could not speak, and the princess became quite worried, for she loved the parrot dearly. She took the bird in her arms and cradled it, stroking its head and wings. This made the prince very happy indeed.

Then the wizard king came in and the prince saw at once how much the princess disliked him. As soon as he had gone – having once again failed to persuade the princess to like him even a little – the prince spoke. "My lady, don't be afraid. I am here to help you."

"What can you do, dear parrot?" cried the princess in astonishment.

"I am not really your parrot," said the prince. "I have come from your mother, the queen." And he took from beneath one wing the miniature portrait which the queen had given him. When she saw it the princess burst out crying again.

"Please don't weep," said the prince. He told her of the fairy and how she had promised to help them. Then he asked if he might take his own shape again. Drying her tears the princess said yes. The parrot pulled one feather from its wing, and there stood the prince in human form. The princess thought she had never seen a more handsome person and she fell in love with him at once.

Meanwhile the fairy prepared a magic chariot, to which she harnessed two mighty eagles. Then she took the parrot from the golden cage and command-ed the bird to take them to the princess.

Thus they passed through the mist quite easily and hovered outside the princess's window. The prince and princess looked out and saw the fairy, and the princess was very happy to see her parrot again. Together they climbed out of the window and got into the chariot. Then the fairy, who was riding on the back of one of the eagles, commanded the great birds to fly back through the mist to the princess's own country.

Meanwhile, the wizard king dreamed that the princess was being carried off. When he woke he went straight to the magic tower and, sure enough, the princess was gone. The wizard king was furious. He went to consult his magic books, and very quickly discovered what had happened. Raging, he

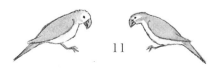

turned himself into a fearsome monster and set off in pursuit. But the fairy sent a powerful wind to slow him down so that the prince and princess arrived safely at the princess's home.

The king and queen greeted them with delight and deep gratitude, but the fairy warned them that the wizard king would soon be there. "The only way to stop him killing you both is to get married at once," the fairy said. The prince and princess were more than willing, and the king and queen kept their promise. So a wedding was quickly celebrated.

But just as the ceremony was ending, the wizard king arrived. He was so angry at the sight of the prince and princess happy together, that he changed back into his human shape and tried to sprinkle some evil black liquid over the bride and groom.

If it had touched them they would have lost their power to move but luckily for them, the fairy made a magical wind that blew the liquid all over the wizard king instead. He fell down in a heap at once, unable to move hand or foot. While he was unconscious, the princess's father ordered that the wizard king be carried away and put in prison.

Now it is well known that wizards lose all their power when they are imprisoned. The wizard king was thus completely helpless, and felt very sorry for himself. The prince took pity on his father and pleaded with the king to set him free. In his gratitude the king agreed and as soon as the doors of the prison were opened, the wizard king flew out in the shape of a strange bird. With a cry he flew off, vowing never to see his son again.

After that everything was very peaceful. The prince and princess settled down together, and in time they ruled the kingdom wisely. They were helped by the fairy, who was persuaded to settle in that land, and who sent for all her books and built a great palace for herself next to that of the prince and princess.

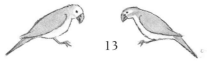

The Partridge Spirit

ALGONQUIN

One red autumn, two brothers went on a hunting expedition for their tribe. They came to the source of the Penobscott river and there they stayed all winter. They had no woman with them to do all the tasks that make a hunter thankful.

So most of the daily tasks fell upon the younger brother who said to his older brother, "I wish there were a woman in our wigwam to mend and cook, to sew and clean for us."

"Well, our mother and sisters are at home, brother. We must do the best we can," replied the older brother. By the time spring came around, their snowshoes were broken and their moccasins were full of holes.

One day, when the snow was still hard and icy, the younger brother came home to find that the wigwam was clean and tidy! A fire was burning and there was hot water already boiling in the pot. He said nothing to his brother, but the next day, he returned home early in order to spy on the wigwam. In the light of the dying sun, he saw a beautiful maiden step through the woods and busy herself about the household tasks.

She was smaller and more delicate than any woman he had ever seen. He stepped into the wigwam and greeted her, "Thank you, maiden, for the work you've been doing. It's very hard for hunters to be alone during the harsh winter."

She replied, "Your brother is coming. I am frightened of him. But I will see you tomorrow if you come home early." With that, she slipped away.

The young hunter said nothing to his brother, but the next day he crept home early and there was the maiden again. Together they played in the snow like children. Just before the sun went down, the young hunter begged her, "Please stay with me forever. My heart was never so happy as now."

The maiden frowned. "Speak to your brother tonight. Tell him everything. Maybe I will stay and serve you both, for I can make snowshoes and moccasins, and build canoes." With that, she slipped away.

When the elder brother came home, he listened eagerly to his young brother, then said, "It seems that we have been lucky! I would be very glad to have a woman help us and care for our camp."

The next morning, the maiden came again. Behind her she pulled a toboggan piled high with hand-sewn garments and finely worked weapons. She greeted both the brothers, who exclaimed at the beauty of the clothes and weapons. "I too am a hunter," was all she would say and she set to work.

The rest of the snowbound spring passed quickly. The maiden cared for the hunters, sewing, mending and making herself use-ful in ways that they both quickly took for granted. They also seemed to be particularly lucky in their hunting. They soon had many furs and were ready to return to their tribe.

When the snow began to thaw, the brothers returned home by canoe down the Penobscott river. When they were halfway down the river the maiden began to look pale and faint. "Stop!" she called out to the hunters. "I can go no further." They sculled to the bank and set her down.

Now although they didn't know it, the maiden had sent out her soul back to the wigwam where they had lived all winter. "Leave me here," she begged. "Say nothing about me to your father, for he would have nothing but scorn for me."

The younger brother was heartbroken. "But I want you to stay with me forever!" He did not realize that the maiden could not come with him because she wasn't a human being at all, but one of the forest spirits.

"It cannot be," replied the maiden. "You must leave me here."

The two brothers returned to their village. When they unpacked the canoe and their family saw the heap of fine furs that they had brought back with them, there was great rejoicing. During the celebrations, the elder brother could not keep quiet about how their luck had changed. He boasted about the strange maiden who had helped them in the depths of the winter.

His father trembled and grew very angry. "All my life I have feared this very thing. My sons, that was no ordinary woman! You have been in the presence of a ghost, a forest spirit, a trickster of the snows! She is a Mikumwess, a witch that can do great harm to human beings."

The elder brother thought to himself, "She may have put a spell upon me. What a fool I've been, not to see it!"

However, the younger brother thought, "Maybe there's something in what father says. Maybe she is a forest spirit. But I didn't feel I was in danger at any time. She was my dearest friend, and I wanted her to be my wife." But he was young and was more inclined to listen to his father's fears than to the wisdom of his own heart.

The father made such a fuss about the maiden being a Mikumwess that the elder brother made a decision. "Come, brother!" he said one day. "Let's go hunting."

Taking some special arrows that were said to be good against witches, the elder brother began to track the maiden. The younger brother didn't know what they were hunting. Suddenly, the elder brother caught sight of the maiden bathing in the stream and drew his bow. At the same time, his brother saw her and started to call and wave to her, but too late! The elder brother's arrow had already flown.

Where the maiden had been swimming was now a confusion of water and feathers. Then they both saw her rise in the shape of a partridge into the sky.

The younger brother's heart was very heavy and he walked silently away. As he was sitting sadly in a birch clearing, a partridge landed at his feet and changed into the maiden. He threw himself at her feet and cried, "Forgive me! I didn't know what my brother intended! I never meant to hunt you, my dearest one!"

"Do not blame yourself," said the maiden. "I know everything. It was not your father's fault either, for he spoke from fear and ignorance. The past is forgotten already. I promise you that the best is yet to come."

And together they played in the woods, as once they had played in the snows, forgetting their sorrows. When the crows flew home to their nests, the young hunter said, "I must return."

The maiden answered, "When you want to see me, come to the woods and I will be here. But, remember, do not marry anyone! Your father has a girl in mind and will speak of marriage soon." And she told him what his father would say, word for word.

He listened carefully, but was not surprised by her words. He knew for certain that she was, indeed, a forest spirit, but he was not afraid.

They kissed gently under the birch trees. "Remember," she reminded him, "if you marry, you will surely die!"

When the young man went home that night, his father spoke, just as the maiden said he would. "My son, I have found a wife for you and the wedding will be this week."

The young hunter nodded and said, "So be it!"

The young bride was brought from her family's wigwam and the wedding feast began. For four days everyone danced and ate and told stories. But on the last day, the young bridegroom began to feel ill. His family laid him upon a white bearskin, but he grew worse and worse. They tried all kinds of remedies to heal him.

But the young hunter's soul yearned for the partridge maiden and as he lay dying, his soul flew out of his body searching for her. At the moment he found her, his soul finally left his body, and they ran together through the woods, never to be parted again.

When his sorrowful family brought the bride to where the young hunter lay, they found that he was already dead. But his face was calm and happy, for he had found his true bride at last.

The Magician's Horse

GREEK

Long, long ago, a king had three sons. One day the three sons went hunting in some woods and the youngest prince became separated from his brothers. They searched for him all day but in the end were forced to return home without him. The prince wandered through the forest for four days, living on roots and berries. Then he came to a great house, hidden among the trees. The door stood wide open, so the prince went inside and looked around. The house was full of wonderful things, but there was no sign of anyone at all.

The prince wandered through the empty rooms until he came to a huge hall. There was a table spread with fine food and wine. The prince sat down and ate and drank his fill. As soon as he was finished, the table and all the food left uneaten vanished away. The prince was astonished by this, but at that moment an old man entered the room. "What are you doing in my house?" he demanded.

"Sir, forgive me," said the prince. "I got lost in the wood and have been wandering for days. If you would take me into your service, I will serve you faithfully."

"Very well," said the old man. "You may serve me. I shall pay you a single gold coin every week. To earn that you must keep the stove in the cellar always lit and care for the black horse which is in my stable. If you do this, there will be food on the table every day and you may eat your fill. Do you agree to this?"

The prince agreed, and so he came to work for the old man who came and went all the time on mysterious errands so that the prince seldom saw him. One day he let the fire in the stove almost die out. The old man came rushing in at the last moment and threw a log on to the fire. "Be more careful," he cried angrily. "If that fire ever goes out you will suffer the consequences."

And so the prince lived in the old man's house for a year and served him faithfully. But he never forgot that he was not really a servant and often thought of his brothers and wondered what they were doing.

Then one day, as he was sitting rather sadly in the stable, he suddenly heard a voice speaking to him. It was the black horse. "Come into my stall," it said. "I have much to tell you."

The prince was astonished. "You can talk!" he cried.

"Of course," said the horse. "I am a magician's horse after all. Oh yes, didn't you know the old man for whom you work is a magician?" The prince confessed that he did not.

"Well," said the horse, "here is what you must do. Fetch my saddle and bridle from that cupboard. Next to them you will find a bottle. The lotion within it will make your hair shine like pure gold." The prince did as he was told and sure enough his hair looked just like gold.

"Now," said the magician's horse, "gather as much wood as you can and fill the stove right to the top." The prince hurried to obey. The stove grew hotter and hotter, and soon flames shot out of it and set fire to the magician's house. The prince hastened back to the stable.

"We do not have long," the horse declared. "Soon the magician will be back. Look in the cupboard again and you will find three things: a mirror, a brush and a whip. Bring them and hurry, for we must be gone." The prince brought the mirror, the brush and the whip and then he mounted the black horse's back and they rode off as fast as the wind.

Before they had gone far the horse's keen ears heard the sounds of pursuit. "Look behind you!" he cried. "What can you see?"

"There is a cloud, like smoke or dust, on the horizon," said the prince.

"That will be the magician," said the horse, and he galloped even faster.

After a while the horse said again, "Look over your shoulder and tell me what you see." The prince did so. The cloud of dust was much nearer.

"Quickly," said the horse, "throw the mirror behind us!" The prince took out the mirror and threw it on the road. There it grew suddenly large. Soon the magician came along, and his horse put its foot on the mirror. The glass gave way with a crack and the horse fell and hurt itself so badly that the magician was forced to walk home, leading his mount.

The prince meanwhile rode on as fast as he could. But soon the black horse's ears began to twitch. "Look behind you," he said. "Tell me what you see."

The prince looked. "I see a cloud of smoke and a tongue of flame."

"That is my master," said the horse. "Be quick and throw the brush behind you." The prince did as he was told and as soon as the brush touched the ground it became a thick and tangled forest. When the magician arrived, on a new horse, he could not get through and was forced to go around the forest.

If the magician had been angry before, now he was furious. He rode so fast that soon he saw the prince in the distance. But the black horse had heard him coming. "Look behind you," he said to the prince. "What do you see?"

"I see a tongue of fire coming closer."

"Then you must throw down the whip," said the horse.

The prince did as he was bidden and as soon as the whip touched the ground it turned into a deep river. The magician rode up to the edge of the river and urged his

mount into it. The water rose higher and higher, until finally it came up so high that it put out the magic fire that was the source of the magician's power. The flame went out with a fizz and the magician vanished, never to be seen again. The black horse slowed to a halt. "We are safe now," he said.

They rode on for a little way until they came to a lake. "See that willow tree?" said the horse. "Gather a branch from it and strike the ground just over there."

The prince did so and a vaulted archway sprang up out of the earth. The prince led the horse through it and found himself in a huge hall.

"I will stay here for a while," said the horse. "But if you want to improve your fortune, you must go on alone until you come to a garden. Within it is a king's palace. Go there and ask to be taken into the king's service. But first of all hide your golden hair under a scarf. Trust me and you will go far. But be sure you do not forget me."

So the prince took his leave of the black horse and went on as he had been instructed. Soon he found himself in a wonderful garden. There he saw the walls and towers of the king's palace. At the gate he met the royal gardener.

"What do you want?" asked the man.

"I want to take service with the king."

"Then you can work for me," said the gardener. "I need someone to sweep the paths and weed the flowerbeds. If you do that you will get a silver penny every day, somewhere to sleep and plenty of food."

So the prince started working in the king's garden. Every day he swept the leaves and pulled up the weeds. And every day he took half the food he was given to the black horse.

One day when they were together after the prince had finished his work, the black horse addressed him. "Tomorrow a number of princes and great lords are coming to the king's castle to woo his three beautiful daughters. They will all stand in a row, and when the three princesses come out they will each be carrying a diamond apple. They will throw these down and

whichever prince's feet they roll to will be that princess's bride. See to it that you are near at hand when this happens. The youngest princess's apple will fall near you. Pick it up quickly and put it in your pocket."

So the prince did as the horse told him. When the royal suitors were gathered, out came the three princesses – and the youngest was, indeed, the fairest of them all. Her apple rolled further than all the rest, and came to the feet of the gardener's boy, who picked it up and put it in his pocket. As he did so the scarf covering his hair slipped, and the princess caught a glimpse of his bright golden hair. "There is more to this young man than I thought," she said to herself. And as she looked at him she felt her heart beat faster.

The king was most unhappy about this turn of events. But he had made the decree that whoever caught the apples would marry the princess who threw them. So three weddings were celebrated. The two older princesses married their noble lords, but the youngest married the gardener's boy and went home with him to the little hut where he lived.

The next day something happened that made the king forget about his youngest daughter's marriage. News came that a neighboring kingdom had declared war. The king prepared for battle at once, and he rode out with the two husbands of his eldest daughters riding at his side. But he was so ashamed of the gardener's boy that he would not even give him a horse to ride with them.

As soon as the army had departed the prince went to where the black horse was stabled. When he told the horse what had happened, the noble beast said at once, "I will carry you to the battle. Fetch my saddle. Also, look in the next room and you will find armor and a sword that you may carry."

So the prince rode forth looking as fine as any noble lord. When he reached the battlefield the king's army was losing. But when the prince joined in, he fought so bravely that the king's fortune changed. The great black horse carried him everywhere, and the prince hewed left and right with his shining sword. Everyone thought he was a great hero who had come to help them. No one recognized the poor gardener's boy.

Towards the end of the battle the prince received a wound in the leg. When the king saw this, he tied up the wound with his own scarf, embroidered with crowns and his royal name. He tried to get the prince to climb onto a litter and be carried home, but the hero climbed onto the back of the black horse, which mounted into the sky and flew away with him!

The prince was soon home and when he had seen that the black horse was safely stabled, he lay down on his bed and fell into an exhausted sleep. There the princess found him. Noticing the bloodsoaked scarf around his leg she looked more closely and saw the king's name upon it. Hearing the victorious army returning, she hurried to fetch her father. When he saw his scarf on the prince's leg he realized at once that it was the gardener's boy who had helped him in battle.

Everyone was overjoyed to discover that the hero of the battle was really a prince, and married to their own princess! The prince told them the whole story, and the black horse was fetched and given a place in the royal stable. After that the prince and princess lived long and happily. The prince often visited the magical horse. They had many more adventures together and remained good friends for the rest of their lives.

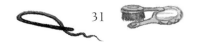

The Witch of Rollright

ENGLISH

In the middle of England, there stands a ring of stones. This is how they came to be standing there.

In the time before this time, there lived a very powerful king over the cold seas. He lived by stealing and killing and he wanted to make all lands his own. He turned his gaze towards England, for he had been told of its rich meadows and fat cattle. He asked his wise men, "How can I become king of this rich country?" The wise men looked into sand and water, into fire and smoke, and said to him, "In the center of England lies a village called Long Compton. Climb the hill above the village, and as soon as you set your eyes upon the village, you will become King of England."

With his men, the king came over the seas in a great ship. As soon as he landed, his soldiers leapt from the ship and began to kill and plunder. No one could stop them and many people fled from their homes.

Word soon came to the people of Long Compton that the king from overseas was advancing towards them. They were very frightened, for they were not skilled in fighting. They gathered together in the village square.

"Someone must stop this king," cried the village elder.

"What will you do, old man?" a woman shouted back. "Shake your stick at him?" The people laughed uneasily, scanning the far hills for signs of the smoke.

"There's only one thing to do," said a young farmer. "We must ask the help of a witch. This kind of force can only be stopped by magic. We are too weak to fight the king."

The crowd was silent. It did seem the best solution, but if they were frightened of the king, they were nearly as scared of witches. So they chose the young farmer to go and find the witch who would stop the foreign king.

Trembling with fear, the farmer went to the lonely cottage on the edge of the village by the crossroads and knocked on the door. Inside lived the oldest witch in the village, a woman so ancient that people had forgotten her real name. She was said to be a powerful enchantress. When they heard snatches of song coming from her window, the people passing by would hurry on again with their fingers in their ears, in case she turned them into something nasty with her spells.

The door opened and there stood the witch. The farmer was quite surprised. He had been expecting a wizened old crone with no teeth. Instead, here was a dark-haired, straight-backed woman. Her deep dark eyes were like wells at midnight.

The farmer stammered, "If you please, wise lady, the villagers of Long Compton need your help. There is a foreign king coming here to make himself King of England. He has no pity for man nor beast, and his men are burning and robbing their way across the land."

"Come in, my good man! I shall help you, if you will help me."

The farmer swallowed hard, and said, "What can I do?"

"Tell the villagers to gather their store of food and put it in a wagon. You are to drive the wagon to where the foreign king and his men are encamped. You must tell him that you bring a feast and the greetings of the people of Long Compton. They will stop and stuff themselves on your provisions, and that will give me time to prepare."

The young farmer quaked in his boots. "But they will kill me!"

"Not if you are steadfast and strong!" said the witch. "Think of your wife and children and the beasts in your fields. Smile and be polite to the visitors. They will take your provisions and leave you alone."

The farmer sighed with relief.

"And one more thing," said the witch. "Bring me a pan of new milk from your best cow. If you perform all these things and trust me, the foreign king shall never rule here."

The farmer nodded and left hastily.

The frightened villagers gladly ransacked their barns and storehouses, bringing out their best food to give to the king's soldiers. Then the farmer set off in his wagon towards their encampment. It was not difficult to find. A smoke trail of destruction hung over the burnt fields and houses. The cruel king was only two villages away. The farmer drove on grimly until the sentries stopped him, thrusting their spears under his chin.

With a glad wave and a smile which did not warm his heart, the farmer leapt down from the wagon and shouted out, "Welcome, followers of the great king. I bring a feast from the people of Long Compton who welcome you to this land!"

The soldiers were astounded. This was the first person not to run away at their approach. The king stepped out of his tent and saw the farmer, who cried out, "Hail, great King of England that shall surely be! The people of Long Compton welcome you and beg that you accept this unworthy feast before you ride further this dark night."

35

The king's mouth curved in a cruel smile. He was well pleased that the village described by his wise men had sent a token of their welcome. He graciously accepted the contents of the wagon and he and his men sat down to enjoy the feast.

The farmer drove away, trembling in every limb at his close escape. He could hear the drunken singing and arguments of the king's men rising raucously into the night behind him.

He had not come within sight of the village when he met with the witch by the roadside. Mindful of his promise, he reached underneath the wagon and handed her the pan of milk. The witch gravely thanked him, and bade him be off. But the farmer left the wagon in a nearby field and crept back in order to see what she would do.

He saw her crouch low to the ground and sing a strange wandering song into the grass at the roadside. Then she poured the milk out onto the road in a circle. The farmer rubbed his eyes for he seemed to see the outlines of many figures singing and dancing, who bowed to the witch as they danced and lapped at the milk. Quickly, he covered his eyes, for the witch was speaking to the fairy folk, and it was not lucky to watch them.

When he awoke in the wet grass, it was morning. Up the hill came the king and his men. The farmer began to curse the witch. She had done

nothing to stop them after all! He was about to pull out his knife and confront them himself, when the witch suddenly appeared in front of the soldiers. She threw back her head with a ringing voice and cried out, "Welcome, mighty king! You have come a long way to meet your destiny."

The king strode towards the witch, "Stand aside, woman! I have come to rule this land."

The witch did not move a muscle. "Indeed, mighty one! But listen to these words of prophecy with care,

> *Seven long strides thou shalt take –*
> *If Long Compton thou canst see*
> *King of England thou shalt be!"*

The king and his men were nearly at the top of the hill; Long Compton was just over the brow. Measuring it with his eyes, the king saw that the seven strides would indeed bring him sight of the village. Thinking to enter the village in triumph, he called for his guard to step forward. Then he took a long step forward, and another and another. He took three strides more, but before he could put down his foot for the last stride, a great mound of earth sprang up across the road, blocking his view.

He cried out with fury, and the witch with glee, for the mound belonged to the fairy folk, who had agreed to help the witch in return for the new milk that the farmer had given her. The witch leapt onto the side of the mound singing,

As Long Compton's hid from thee,
King of England thou shalt not be!
Rise up stick, and stand still stone,
King of England thou shalt be none.
Thou and thy men here stones shall be
And I myself an elder tree!

The king staggered; then he was rooted to the spot. In the time it takes to count to three, the guards halted in their tracks and fused together in a huddle of stones, some standing, some crouching with their hands over their heads, some lying on the ground in terror.

The witch saw the farmer open-mouthed with wonder and said to him, "Run home and tell the villagers that they are safe. I shall keep watch over these villains, never fear." And with those words, she began to grow brown and green and white, as she turned slowly into an elder tree. The farmer ran home to Long Compton with the good news, but he never meddled with magic again.

The village called this circle of stones "The Rollrights." And if you go there today, you will see where King Stone stands alone, and where the guards huddle together as the Whispering Knights. But though you may seek to count the stones and see how many soldiers there were in that army, the number will be different every time you try. And be sure to curtsy to the elder tree which stands near the village, for the Witch of Rollright still keeps her careful watch.

Ivan and the Wizard

RUSSIAN

An old man and an old woman had a son they loved very much. But the couple were very poor and the old man decided to apprentice his son to a master. That way he could learn a trade and be able to make his way in the world, and he could look after his parents as they grew older still.

So the old man set out for the city with his son and tried to find him a master. But no matter how many people he asked – bakers, wheelwrights, blacksmiths, barrelmakers, tanners and weavers – he could find no one who would give his son a place. All of them wanted money and the old man had nothing to pay them with. And so the two returned home sadly, and the old man and the old woman wept loud and long. But their son, whose name was Ivan, told them to cheer up. "For," he said, "we can try again tomorrow in another part of the city."

So the old man and the old woman dried their tears and the next day the old man set out again for the city, with Ivan by his side. But no matter how many people the old man spoke to, no one wanted to apprentice his son.

Then, at the end of the day, as they were preparing to return home again, a tall, well-dressed man came up to the old father and asked him why he looked so sad.

"I have been looking everywhere for someone who will take my son as an apprentice but no one wants to take him on without payment, and I have no money."

"Well," said the stranger, looking at Ivan, "give him to me. In three years I will teach him many wonderful things. But remember this, you must be at this very spot exactly three years from now, not a minute earlier or a minute later. Otherwise you will not get your son back."

The old man was so overjoyed that he forgot to ask the stranger's name, or where he lived, or even what he would teach Ivan. He gave his son over into the man's keeping and went home happily to tell his wife all about their good fortune. But what he did not know was that the man to whom he had apprenticed his son was a wizard.

Three years passed quickly. By that time the old man had completely forgotten the day and the hour that he was supposed to be back in the city to collect his son. But one day, shortly before the end of the three years, a strange bird alighted on a mound of earth next to the old man's house and turned into a handsome young man.

Of course, it was Ivan. He had come to remind his parents that the three years were up on the next day and that the old man must go to the city and be at a certain place at a certain time.

"But," Ivan said, "there are some things you should know. I am not my master's only apprentice. There are eleven others and he does not want to give any of us up. In fact, the others have been with him forever because when their parents came to claim them they could not recognize their children at all. If you don't recognize me tomorrow, I shall be forced to stay as well."

"I shall have no difficulty in recognizing my own son," said the father.

"It will not be as easy as that," said Ivan. "You see, our master is really a wizard, and he will make us all look exactly alike. And what is more, he will put us into other shapes, to make it even harder."

"What shall I do then?" cried the old man.

"Listen to me and all shall be well," said Ivan. "First of all my master will show you twelve white doves. And every one will look exactly the same, feather for feather, as the next. He will ask you which one is me. Watch carefully because, as the doves fly overhead, I shall fly just a little bit higher than the rest. And so you will know it is me."

"I shall not forget," said the old man.

"But that is not the end of it," said Ivan, "for my master will next lead out twelve horses, every one the same from mane to tail. And

again, he will ask you to show him which one is your son. Watch carefully, because I shall stamp my right foot twice as you go past, and so you will know that it is me."

"Be sure I shall remember that," said his father.

"There is more yet," said Ivan. "Next my master will bring out twelve youths, and every one of them will look just the same, as though they had one mother. Look very carefully at each one of them. You will see that on the right cheek of one of them is a fly. That one will be me."

"I will do as you say," promised the old man. With that, the youth went outside and struck the mound of earth with his right foot. At once he turned back into a bird and flew away.

The next day the old man went into the city and at the appointed time he was waiting at the exact same spot where he had first met the wizard three years ago. And there, sure enough, came the tall, well-dressed man.

"Good day to you, old man," he said. "I have taught your son many wonderful things, just as I promised. But if you want him back you must recognize him. If you do not, he will have to stay with me forever." Then, just as Ivan had said he would, the wizard set free twelve white doves, every one of them alike in every way.

"Now show me your son," said the wizard.

The old man looked and looked, and every one of the birds seemed exactly the same. Then he noticed that one of them was flying a little bit higher than all the rest. "That is my son," he said.

The wizard looked angry. "Well," he said, and snapped his fingers. There, in place of the twelve white doves, were twelve identical horses, every one of them as handsome and high stepping as the other. "Which one of these is your son?" asked the wizard.

The old man looked and looked. He walked up the line of horses, and he walked down. Then he saw that one of them stamped its right foot twice on the ground, and he went up to that one and touched its mane. "This is my son," he said.

"Well, well, well," said the wizard, looking even more angry. He snapped his fingers and in the place of the twelve horses stood twelve young men, dressed in fine silk and linen and every one of them as alike as though they had been born to the same mother. "And which one of these is your son?"

The old man walked up the line and down the line. Then he walked down the line and up the line. The wizard tapped his foot. The old man peered closely at every identical face until he saw that one of them had a fly on his right cheek. He stopped in front of that youth. "This is my son," he said.

The wizard stamped his foot and vanished in a flash of light and a curl of smoke. Eleven of the youths vanished too, leaving the old man standing in the road with his son by his side. Joyfully they embraced and set off home together.

They lived a happy life together, and with the magic he had learned from the wizard, Ivan earned them some money. But it was still not much, and so one day the boy said to his father, "I'm going to turn myself into a bird. Take me to market and sell me for the best price you can get. But don't sell the cage I shall be in, or I won't be able to get back."

Then he stamped on the earth with his right foot and became a bird in a beautiful golden cage. The old man went to market and soon had a crowd of people who wanted to buy the bird. Then the wizard appeared and offered more than anyone.

The old man agreed, but took the bird from its cage. The wizard scowled mightily at this, and wrapped the bird in his handkerchief. Then he went home and called to his lovely daughter. "Come and see what I have for you," he cried. "It's that rascal who used to be my apprentice."

The wizard's daughter, who had taken a liking to Ivan, came running. "Where is he?" she asked. But when the wizard unfolded his handkerchief

the bird was nowhere to be found.

The next week as market day approached, Ivan said, "I am going to turn myself into a horse. Take me to the market and sell me for the best price you can get. But be sure you keep my bridle, because otherwise I shall not be able to get back."

Then he stamped on the earth with his right foot and in a flash there stood a great wild black horse with the most wonderful jeweled bridle. The old man took him to market and soon a crowd gathered. Some offered one thing and some another, but soon the wizard arrived and he offered more than anyone. The old man took the money and began to take off the horse's bridle.

"Wait," said the wizard. "How shall I lead my horse without a bridle?" The old man hesitated. But all the other horse dealers began to shout that he could not sell a horse without a bridle. What could he do? He gave the bridle to the wizard.

Smiling, the wizard went home, leading the horse. He took it to his stable and tethered it so tightly that it could not even move its head to eat or drink. The wizard went inside his house and called to his daughter. "Come and see what I have caught," he said.

"What is it?" asked the girl.

"None other than that rascal who used to be my apprentice." The girl went out to the stable to look. But when she saw the horse tied up so tightly she took pity on it and loosened the reins. At once the horse pulled free and galloped off. The girl ran indoors, weeping. "I'm sorry, father. The horse has run away."

The wizard gave a great cry and turned himself into a grey wolf. He ran as fast as the wind and faster yet after the horse, and soon he almost caught up with it. The horse came to the bank of a river and, quick as a flash, turned into a perch and swam off. But the wizard turned himself into a great greedy pike with savage teeth and swam after it as fast as the wind and faster.

The perch swam and swam until it was exhausted. Then it came to the bank where some lovely maidens were washing clothes. The perch jumped out of the water and became a golden ring which rolled to the feet of one of the maidens.

The wizard took his own shape again and demanded the golden ring. The maiden threw it on the ground and when it struck the earth it shattered. And instead of the ring were several grains of wheat. The wizard laughed and turned himself into a cock. He began to peck at the wheat. Then one of the grains became a hawk, and it tore the cock to pieces.

And that was the end of the wizard.

As for Ivan, he went home and continued to make his old parents rich. And I did hear that he married the wizard's daughter, but whether that is true or not, I cannot say.

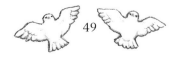

The Boy Magician

HOPI

In the heart of a wilderness, there once lived an old woman and her young grandson. Both of the boy's parents were dead, but from his father he had inherited some magical skills, so that his grandmother used to call him "my young magician." They were happy enough in their life together. By day, the old woman would be busy with cooking and cleaning, while the young boy went hunting to catch food for their table.

Often the grandmother would talk about the time when the boy would be ready to go out into the world. "Always go to the east," she would say. "Never go to the west, for that way lies danger." But no matter how often the boy asked her, she would never say what kind of danger lay to the west. And as he grew older and stronger the boy thought that one day he would have to go and find out for himself.

One day the old woman said again, "Never go to the west." But this time her grandson – who was by now a young man – would not rest until he had an answer from her. At last, reluctantly, she said, "There is a creature out there. A terrible creature. It wants to do harm to everyone who sees it.

If you were to go near it, we should both be killed." More than that she would not say, but her words only made the young man want to go and find out about this creature. He trusted his strength and skill and his knowledge of magic, to keep both himself and his grandmother safe.

And so, when he set out next morning to go hunting, as soon as he was out of sight of his grandmother's lodge, he turned west. All day he traveled and saw nothing. Then he came to the edge of a lake, where he decided to rest. He had not been there long when he suddenly heard a strange voice. "I see you," said the voice.

The boy looked all around him and at the sky, but he could see no one. "Where are you?" he asked.

"Where you cannot see me," answered the voice. Then it said, "I am going to send a hurricane. It will smash your grandmother's house to pieces. How do you like that?"

"Why, thank you," said the boy. "We are always needing firewood. Now we shall have plenty."

"Go home," said the voice. "I dare say you won't like it that much."

So the boy hurried home. When he was almost in sight of the lodge a great wind blew up from nowhere. It rooted trees out of the ground and threw rocks about as though they were pebbles. The boy's grandmother looked out and saw him coming. "Quickly," she cried. "Get inside before you are killed."

As soon as he was inside the old woman began to scold him. "You have been to the west," she said. "Now we are both going to die."

"Don't worry, grandmother," said the boy. "I shall use my magic to turn the walls of the lodge to stone." He spoke some magic words and though the hurricane blew as strongly as it could, it could not even move the stone lodge. When it had blown itself out, the old woman and the boy went outside and found enough firewood to last them for a month.

The next day the boy was ready to go to the west again. But his grandmother begged and pleaded with him until he promised to go east instead. He set out that way, but soon his feet turned west again and he found himself back at the lake. He looked all around and could see nothing. Then he heard the strange voice again. "I'm going to send a great storm of hail to destroy your grandmother's lodge. What do you think of that?"

"I should like that," said the boy. "I need some new spears."

"Go home then," said the voice,"but I don't think you'll be so pleased."

The boy hurried home and, just as he was nearing his grandmother's lodge, the sky got very dark. Huge hailstones the size of boulders began to fall out of the sky. The boy ran as fast as he could and got safely into the lodge where his grandmother waited. "Now we shall surely die," the old woman cried.

But once again the boy used his magic and turned the walls of the lodge to stone. The hailstones banged and rattled against them, bouncing off harmlessly. When the storm was over, the boy came out of the lodge and saw that there were dozens of sharp, glittering spearheads sticking in the ground. He ran to get poles to fit them to. But when he returned the spearheads had vanished. "Where are all my beautiful spears?" he demanded.

"They have all melted away," said his grandmother. "They were only made of ice." The boy was very disappointed. He began to wonder how he could get his revenge on the owner of the voice. "Don't be so foolish," his grandmother said. "Take my advice and leave well alone."

But the boy was determined to be avenged. He took a special stone that was full of magic and hung it around his neck on a thong. Then he set off back to the lake. This time he went as stealthily as he could and, when he arrived at the lake, he crouched down behind a big rock and looked carefully around him.

At first he saw nothing, then, as he was watching, he saw a horrible head pop up out of the middle of the lake. It had a face not only on the front, but on the sides and back as well. Eight eyes, eight ears, four noses, four mouths. "I see you," cried the youth. Then he said, "How would you like it if this lake dried up?"

"Nonsense," said the ugly head, speaking out of all four of its mouths. "That could never happen."

"Go home and see," shouted the boy, imitating the head. Then he took the stone from around his neck and threw it up into the air. As it went up it got bigger and bigger, and when it fell in the lake it made a great splash. At once the water began to boil and bubble and the head made a great roaring sound.

The boy ran away home as fast as he could and told his grandmother what had happened. "It's no good," she said. "Others have tried to kill him, but they have all died."

Nonetheless the boy decided to go back to the lake the next day. When he arrived he found the lake had boiled away entirely and that all the creatures in it were dead – except for a big green frog that was hopping weakly about in the middle. The boy looked at it and knew that this was what the creature that had plagued him was really like. He took a big stick and went to kill it.

"Please spare me," cried the frog in a little voice, not at all like the one it had used to terrify so many people. But the boy thought of all those who had been killed by the monster, and he struck the frog with his stick and killed it. Then he went home and told his grandmother all that had happened.

After that they lived in peace, and now the old woman calls her grandson "my great big magician," because of the good use to which he had put his magic.

The Wizard Who Got Sick

ARMENIAN

There was once a wizard who grew sick. Every medicine he tried made him feel worse and so he consulted his magic books. There he found it written that travel might be good for him, so he decided to go out and wander the world until he felt better.

On the first day he came to where a fountain of fresh water bubbled up out of the earth. A number of women from a nearby village were filling their water jars and washing their clothes in the fountain. The wizard walked up to the women and asked if he could have some of the water to drink for he was hot and thirsty.

"Not if you turned to dust before my eyes," said one of the women. And the rest were all as rude and unfriendly. All except for one, who looked kindly at the thirsty wizard and said to her companions, "We can spare a drop of water for a poor man."

As the wizard drank deeply she said, "There is a corner of our barn ready for you if you would like to sleep there tonight." The wizard thanked her for her kindness and went home with her.

56

The woman's husband met them at the door. "Who is this you have brought home?" he asked.

"A stranger," said the woman, "and our guest this night."

"Then come in and be welcome," said the man. "I will set the table."

"I'm afraid I only eat freshly killed beef," said the wizard, who had noticed that they had a single cow tied up next to their house.

"Then I shall go and kill the cow," said the man without hesitation. "Only the best is good enough for a guest." That evening they all ate well, and the wizard went off to sleep in the barn. As he left the house he heard the woman saying quietly to her husband that she did not know how they would manage now that the cow was gone.

Next morning the couple were woken by the sound of a cow lowing outside.

"What can that be?" asked the woman.

"I don't know," said the man. "We only had one cow and we ate that last night." They went outside and there to their amazement was their own cow, hale and hearty as ever, and very much alive.

But there was no sign of their guest.

Meanwhile the wizard went on his way and, as the sun rose high in the sky, he met a man gathering brushwood. "Ho, brother, you won't grow fat that way," said the wizard.

"What more can I do," answered the man. "There's no other work for me."

The wizard waved a hand and the dry twigs and branches became a thriving vineyard, full of ripe grapes ready for picking and making into wine. "May you prosper, brother," said the wizard and he went on his way.

Further along the road he saw a man walking sadly among a grove of dead trees. "Hey, that's a fine orchard you have there!" cried the wizard. And sure enough, the trees were suddenly heavy with fruit. "Prosper and be well, brother," said the wizard and he went on his way.

Next he saw a man carrying rocks on his back. "That's a fine herd of sheep you have there, my friend," said the wizard. At once all the rocks turned into fat sheep. "May you prosper always," cried the wizard and he went on his way.

For a whole year he traveled about doing deeds of this kind, until he was completely cured of his sickness. Then he decided to return the way he had come and see how the people he had helped were faring.

First he came back to the man whose stones he had turned into sheep. The man had slaughtered all the beasts and was having a huge feast. "Can you spare some of that delicious looking meat for me?" asked the wizard.

"Be off with you," shouted the man. "Did you help me look after the sheep?"

"Give me at least a morsel, for the sake of charity," said the wizard. But the man only shouted at him to go away. The wizard waved his hands and the roasting sheep turned back into stones.

Then he went on his way until he came to the orchard, where men were busy picking fruit. "May I have an apple?" asked the wizard.

"Clear off!" shouted the owner of the orchard. "We don't want your sort here." The wizard gestured with both hands and the trees became as barren as they had been before he had caused them to flower and bear fruit.

The wizard went on his way again, until he came to the vineyard. "May I have some of your grapes?" he asked one of the workers.

"I'll ask the master," said the man.

He soon came back, shaking his head. "The master says he'll not give you a single grape." The wizard raised a hand and the vineyard vanished. A bundle of dead twigs lay on the ground in its place.

Again the wizard went on until he came to the house where the man and woman lived who had killed their only cow to feed him. The couple came to the door, smiling and happy to see him.

"How good it is to see you again," said the man.

"May we offer you something for your journey?" said the woman.

The wizard smiled. "Truly you are good people," he said. "For all the good you have done and for your kindness to me I will reward you. Every morning you shall find four hundred gold coins under your bed. May you always prosper." With these words he vanished.

The couple were very glad with their newfound fortune, and you may be sure they lived very happily after that time.

As for the wizard, he went home and lived on for many years. And whenever he felt sick or low in spirits he would go and visit the couple who had offered him such kindness, and they would sit and talk of the ways of the world until the fire went out in the hearth.

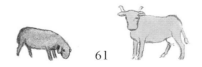

Pome and Peel

ITALIAN

Once upon a time a noble lord and his lady longed to have a child but no matter how much they wished, they were unlucky. So the lord decided to visit a certain wizard he knew of to ask for his help. The wizard gave him an apple. "Give this to your wife to eat," he said, "and you will soon have a fine son."

The lord took the apple home and told his wife what the wizard had said. The lady was delighted and sent for her maid to peel the apple. The maid did so, but instead of throwing the peel away, she ate it.

Which is why, nine months later, a son was born to both the lady and to the maidservant, on the same day and at the same time. The lord looked at them both and saw that they were as alike as alike, save that the maid's child had a skin as red and bright as shiny peel, while his own wife's child had skin as white as the pulp of an apple. And so he named them Pome and Peel, and decided to bring them both up as his own sons.

The two boys grew to manhood like brothers. Then one day they heard about a wizard's daughter, who was said to be more beautiful than the morning star. But no one had ever seen her because the wizard protected her and never allowed her to go out of his house.

"How can we get to see this wonderful girl?" said Pome.

"I have an idea," said Peel. "Let's build a horse of bronze and hide inside it."

So that is what they did. They took the bronze horse to the wizard's house and climbed inside its hollow belly with a violin and a flute. Then they began to play. The wizard looked out of his window and saw the marvelous creature that seemed to be making music all on its own. Immediately, the wizard went out and brought the bronze horse inside.

He called to his daughter, "Come and see what I have found for you." And the maiden came from her room to look at the horse and was quite delighted. She sat down to listen to the music while the wizard went about his own business. But as soon as the wizard had gone, out jumped Pome and Peel.

The wizard's daughter was frightened at first, but Pome said, "Don't be afraid. We won't hurt you. We heard all about your beauty and we wanted to see for ourselves." And Peel said, "We can go right away, but if you like our music, we can keep playing for a while. Then we'll go and no one need ever know we were here."

First, that she would see three horses, one red, one white and one black. Then, since she loved horses more than anything, she would jump on the back of the white one, which would run off with her and throw her over a cliff onto some rocks.

Second, that she would see three dogs, one red, one white, one black, and that she would pick up the black dog, which would tear out her throat.

Third, that on the first night she spent with her husband, a great snake would come in through the window of their room and destroy them both.

The wizard's daughter smiled shyly and asked them to play some more for her. And, by the time they had spent several hours together, she did not want them to go at all. Indeed she had fallen in love with Pome, and when he suggested that she come with them, she agreed at once. They all got inside the bronze horse and rolled it outside the wizard's house and so escaped entirely unseen.

When the wizard came home he looked high and low for his daughter. When he could find no sign of her, he consulted his magic books and quickly learned what had happened. The wizard was beside himself with rage. He rushed upstairs, leaned out of the window and screamed three curses after his daughter. This is what they were.

Now it happened that three fairies were passing below the window at that moment, and so they heard everything. Later on that night they stopped at an inn and there they saw the wizard's daughter, with Pome and Peel, sleeping beside the fire.

"My goodness," said one of the fairies. "They wouldn't sleep so soundly if they knew what was in store for them." Now Peel wasn't actually asleep at all, and so he overheard everything the three fairies said. First they talked about the three horses.

"If only someone were there when it happened, he could cut off the white horse's head. Then everything would be all right," said the first fairy.

"And if only someone were there when she meets the dogs he could cut off the black one's head. Then that would be all right," said the second fairy.

"And if only someone were there when the snake comes through the window, he could cut off its head. Then everything would be all right," said the third fairy.

"Except," said the first fairy, "if anyone were to breathe a word about this, they would turn to stone at once."

Peel lay quiet and thought about all he had heard. He knew everything

66

that was going to happen to Pome and the wizard's daughter but he did not
dare speak of it for fear of turning to stone. Then he thought how much he
loved his brother, and how fair the wizard's daughter was, and he decided to
do what he could to help anyway.

Next morning they set out along the way. Pome had already sent word
home to his father and in a while they met a messenger who had brought
three horses for them to ride. The wizard's daughter immediately jumped on
the back of the white horse, but Peel drew his sword and, with one blow, cut
off its head.

"What are you doing? Have you gone mad?" cried the wizard's daughter.

Peel shook his head. "I cannot tell you," he said.

Then the wizard's daughter turned to Pome. "Your brother has an evil
heart. I do not want to travel any further with him." But Peel swore that he
had acted in a moment of madness and begged her to forgive him.

They rode on until they came in sight of Pome and Peel's house. There
three little dogs ran out to greet them, one red, one white, and one black. The
wizard's daughter bent to pick up the black one, but Peel drew his sword and
cut off its head with a single blow. "Monster!" cried the wizard's daughter.
"Why are you so cruel?"

Again Peel said nothing. Then Pome's parents came out and did their best to make peace between them. They persuaded the wizard's daughter that Peel must have suffered a fit of madness. They all went inside and the wedding of Pome and the wizard's daughter was celebrated.

But during the great feast that followed Peel hardly said a word to anyone. To everyone who asked he said that he felt fine and that nothing was the matter. Then he excused himself and went off to bed early. But instead of going to his own room, he went into the bridal chamber and hid under the bed. Soon the couple arrived and got into bed. When they were asleep Peel crept out and drew his sword. In a little while, the window opened and in slithered a huge snake. With a cry Peel leapt upon it and cut off its head with a single blow.

Woken by the noise Pome and his bride sat up in bed and saw Peel with his drawn sword. But the snake had vanished the moment its head was cut off, so they thought that he was about to attack them. "Call the guards!" shouted Pome, while the wizard's daughter cried out that she had forgiven Peel twice now but this time he should be put in prison and then executed.

So Peel was seized and thrown into a dungeon to await his death. Realizing that he was doomed anyway, he sent a message to the wizard's daughter, begging her to visit him in prison. Reluctantly, she came. Peel looked at her sadly. "Do you remember," he said, "that day when we stopped at an inn to rest?"

"Of course."

"Well, while you and Pome were asleep three fairies came in. I overheard them talking and they said that your father had placed three curses upon you. The first was that when you saw three horses you would get on the white one and that it would cause your death. But if someone were to cut its head off then everything would be well. Except that if anyone breathed a word of this they would turn to stone."

Even as he said this Peel's feet and legs turned to marble. "Stop!" cried the wizard's daughter.

But Peel said, "I am doomed anyway." And he told her about the curse of the three dogs. As he spoke his body turned to marble up to the neck.

"I understand. I forgive you," cried the wizard's daughter. "Please don't say anymore!"

But Peel, speaking with difficulty, told her of the snake. As he did so, he fell silent and in his place stood a marble statue.

"Alas!" said the wizard's daughter. "Poor Peel, what have I done!" Then she thought, "There is only one person who can undo this terrible wrong and that is my father." And she took pen and ink and paper and wrote a letter to him, begging his forgiveness and asking him to come to her as quickly as possible. When he received her letter the wizard came at once, for indeed he loved his daughter more than anything.

As soon as he arrived the wizard's daughter ran straight to him and flung her arms about his neck. "Oh, Father," she said, "I am sorry for making you angry. But I really do love Pome and we are very happy."

"What do you want of me?" said her father.

"There is only one thing that makes me sad," and she took him to the statue of Peel. "This good youth was only trying to help. Please will you bring him back to life?"

The wizard sighed. "Very well," he said, "I will do this for you." He took a phial of liquid from a pocket in his robes and let a little of it fall onto the statue. At once, Peel sprang up alive again and there was great rejoicing. And when the wizard saw Pome and Peel together, he recognized them as the children of the lord and lady he had helped long ago by giving them a magic apple. Then he was truly sorry for all that he had done and thereafter everyone lived very happily for the rest of their days.

The Story of Merlin

WELSH

It all began with dragons.

Long ago in Britain there lived a king named Vortigern. He was not a good man and no one really liked him. In fact, they said that he had stolen the crown and that the real king was named Ambrosius the Golden. But no one knew where he was – until one day a huge army showed up off the shores of Britain, and its leader, who said that he was Ambrosius, told everyone that he had come to claim back the kingdom.

When he heard this, Vortigern grew fearful. He summoned his wizards and asked them what he should do. "There is only one way to escape Ambrosius," said the chief wizard. "You must build a new castle and stay in it until he goes away."

"Where shall I build this castle?" asked Vortigern.

The chief wizard thought for a moment. Then he pointed to a tall hill on the horizon. "There," he said.

Vortigern sent for his builders and told them to make him a strong castle on top of the hill. To begin with everything was fine. The builders dug huge

foundations and dragged massive blocks of stone up the hillside. The walls began to grow upwards until they were nearly as high as a tall man. And then, during the night, they fell down. In the morning the builders came to admire their work, but the great stone blocks were rolled about all over the hillside like giant square marbles. "Earthquake," said the head builder. "That's what it was. You'll see." So they set about building the walls again and by nightfall they were back in place. Then the builders went off to bed, satisfied they had done a good job.

But the next morning the stones were scattered all over the hillside again. And this time the earth was all dug up around them as though someone with very large feet had walked about, kicking the stones. Now the builders were really worried, so they sent a message to King Vortigern. When he heard what had happened, he sent for his wizards.

finished as soon as possible.

The captain gathered his best men and told them to ride north, south, east and west and every direction in between, until they found a boy without a father.

In the end, it was the captain himself who found the boy.

He was riding through a little town not far from the hill where Vortigern was trying to build his castle, when he saw some boys fighting. One of the boys broke away from the rest and ran off. As he did so, the others shouted after him, "Emrys has no father! Emrys has no father!"

"Ah," said the chief wizard, stroking his long white beard and looking wise. "It's obvious that some evil spirit is at work here. It must be knocking down the walls every night."

"What shall I do?" said Vortigern.

"Well," answered the chief wizard. "You must find a boy who has no father. And when you find him you must kill him and sprinkle his blood on the stones. That will do it."

Vortigern sent for the captain of his soldiers and told him to go and look for a boy without a father at once because Ambrosius and his army were getting closer, and Vortigern needed to have his new castle

At once, the captain rode after the boy. When he caught up with him he called out, "Boy! Wait! Is it true? Do you really have no father?" The boy stopped and looked up at the captain on his tall horse. He had one blue eye and one green. He nodded.

"Then you must come with me," said the captain.

"I will," said the boy, and climbed up in front of the captain. He said nothing at all on the way to the hill. When they arrived they found that Vortigern himself, and his wizards, were already there.

"Is this the boy?" demanded the king.

"It is," said the captain, saluting. Vortigern looked at the boy.

"What is your name?" he asked.

"Emrys," said the boy.

Vortigern looked at his wizards, who nodded. "Proceed," said the king.

"I know you want to kill me," said the boy called Emrys, "but I know the real reason why your castle will not stand."

"What's that?" said Vortigern.

"There is a lake of water under the hill," said the boy. "Under the water

there is a stone chest with a lid." He looked at Vortigern's wizards. "Do you know what is inside the chest?" he asked.

The wizards scratched their heads and tugged at their beards and shifted from one foot to the other. But not one of them said anything. "Well?" said Vortigern.

"Inside the chest are two dragons," said the boy. "Every night they come out and fight in the lake. Their fighting shakes the earth and makes the walls of your castle fall down. If you don't believe me tell your builders to dig down into the hill."

Vortigern gave the order and the builders began to dig. The hole got deeper and deeper until they revealed a lake of still, dark water. Then they brought pumps and engines and began to drain the lake. Soon the water was almost gone and everyone could see the top of a huge stone chest.

Vortigern's builders brought a crane and some ropes and very slowly they lifted off the lid. Inside, curled up, sleeping, were two dragons. One was red and the other white. They woke up. They crawled out of the stone chest and stretched their wings.

77

King Vortigern, his wizards and all the builders and soldiers drew back in fear. The boy did not move.

Then the two dragons flew up into the air and began to fight with each other. The noise was like thunder and lightning and wind all at once. At last, the white dragon began to grow tired. The red dragon bit it on the neck and then it breathed out some fire. The white dragon fell to the ground and you could hear the crash a hundred miles away. The red dragon flew away.

Everyone was silent on the hillside. King Vortigern looked at the boy. "How did you know about the dragons?" he asked.

"I know many things," answered the boy. "I know that King Ambrosius the Golden is coming with a great army, and that he will soon be here. And I know that you are going be killed, just like the white dragon."

With that, the boy vanished, leaving the king and his wizards and all his men very much afraid. And everything the boy had said would happen did happen. King Ambrosius came with his army and Vortigern was killed in the battle that followed. His castle never did get finished. In fact, you can still see the ruins today, if you can find the hill.

As for the boy named Emrys, he grew up to become the greatest wizard that ever lived. But he was not called Emrys any longer. Everyone called him Merlin, and he was King Arthur's magician. And everyone said he was the wisest man who ever lived.

Sources for the Stories

The Wizard King

I love the way this story preserves the age-old rivalry between the fairy people, who inherit their magic, and the wizards, who learn theirs as apprentices. I first read it in one of the great collections of fairy tales compiled by Andrew Lang in the nineteenth century. Lang gives his source as the *Cabinet de Fées* ("The Fairy Box") one of the most famous collections of French folktales — J. M.

The Partridge Spirit

This tale was collected by the folklorist Charles Leland in 1884. The taboo against mortals marrying other unworldly beings is very strong in most cultures: usually such marriages are either of short duration or require the mortal partner (as here) to leave human life and join this otherworldly love — C. M.

The Magician's Horse

This story from modern-day Greece still manages to preserve some elements of its classical heritage. The story of the three princesses with their diamond apples probably goes back to the judgement of Paris, the root cause of the Trojan war. Talking horses are a common feature of folk tales, and I rather liked that it was the horse that is the hero here, rather than the magician himself — J. M.

The Witch of Rollright

The legend surrounding my nearest stone circle, the Rollright Stones, is fragmentary. Local people tell stories about the fairies at Rollright and I fell to wondering what part they played in its origin. This story is the result of my pondering, which felt rather like tuning into an old story that the stones themselves still remembered — C. M.

Ivan and the Wizard

Versions of this story are to be found all over the world. I have found English, French, German and Swiss versions, but none as good or varied as this Russian tale, which appears in a number of collections. The theme of the chase, and the transformations of the wizard and his apprentice, appear in a variant form in the Welsh tale of Taliesin — J.M.

The Boy Magician

Versions of this Hopi story are told all over the United States. I particularly liked this one, which I heard while visiting friends in New Mexico. It belongs to the Hopi people, whose traditions are still very much alive today — J. M.

The Wizard Who Got Sick

This wonderful story from Armenia was told to me by a peasant woman named Gyuli Avagian in 1950, though it has probably been circulating for a lot longer than that. The idea of the wizard who goes about doing good deeds is an interesting variant on the more negative side of wizardry that is found in many folk stories — J. M.

Pome and Peel

This story combines lots of wonderful elements: the magical birth of the two heroes, the trick by which they get into the magician's house, the triple cures and the fairy helpers who happen to be in the right place at the right time. It comes from the Umbrian region of Italy, where stories of resourceful heroes and heroines are still told to this day — J. M.

The Story of Merlin

This story makes its first recorded appearance in *The History of The Kings of Britain* by Geoffrey of Monmouth, written in the twelfth century. It was the first book to tell the story of King Arthur from birth to death, and it became a best-seller of the time. The story of Merlin was originally attached to an older figure called Emrys or Ambrosius — J. M.

BAREFOOT BOOKS publishes high-quality picture books for children of all ages and specializes in the work of artists and writers from many cultures. If you have enjoyed this book and would like to receive a copy of our current catalog, please write to our New York office: Barefoot Books, 41 Schermerhorn Street, Suite 145, Brooklyn, New York, NY 11201-4845 email: sales@barefoot-books.com   website: www.barefoot-books.com